O'BRIEN flyers

FLYER books are for confident readers
who can take on the challenge of
a longer story.

D1320133

Can YOU spot the aeroplane
hidden in the story?

FOR SALE
and also for Susannah

CONOR McHALE was born in Dublin in 1969. Shortly before leaving school, he decided he would study to be an archaeologist. This decision caused his father to roar with laughter. After ten years working in Irish archaeology, Conor has only just realised what the joke was. He lives in Dublin with his wife, Susannah, and their son, Oscar. He loves Rembrandt, hates celery and often loses his keys.

Jigsaw Stew

Conor McHale

THE O'BRIEN PRESS
DUBLIN

First published 2000 by The O'Brien Press Ltd,
12 Terenure Road East, Rathgar, Dublin 6, Ireland.
Tel. +353 1 4923333; Fax. +353 1 4922777
E-mail books@obrien.ie
Website www.obrien.ie
Reprinted 2002, 2004, 2008.

ISBN: 978-0-86278-688-5

British Library Cataloguing-in-Publication Data.
McHale, Conor
Jigsaw stew. - (O'Brien flyers ; bk 6)
1.Children's stories
I.Title
823.9'14[J]

4 5 6 7 8 9
08 09 10 11 12 13

The O'Brien Press receives assistance from

Editing, typesetting, layout, design: The O'Brien Press Ltd
Illustrations: Conor McHale
Printing: Cox & Wyman Ltd

Chapter 1

Making a Meal of it 7

Chapter 2

Jigsalgia attacks! 18

Chapter 3

The Cardboard Snow Boat 30

Chapter 4

The Mulgrew Mix-up 42

Chapter 5

Cured? 56

Making a Meal of it

An icy wind blew. It shook trees and rattled gates. It whistled under the **armpits** of snowmen.

Jack MacAnoolie stared out and sighed. He was tired of being inside. For over a month now the weather had trapped him and his family indoors.

Jack's sister Molly was passing the time by calling him names.

That was bad enough, but they had run out of **food** too.

To stay alive, they were eating old leather boots boiled (with a little salt) until they were chewable.

Jack's mother was a resourceful cook. But soon the boot cupboard ran dry. So Mrs MacAnoolie needed new ingredients.

She looked around the cottage
until her eyes came to rest on a chair.
'That looks **delicious**,' she said. It
went into the pot with a splash.

After that everything and anything
was cooked. Bicycles, books,
candlesticks and doorknobs.

One day she made a pot of
stew using an old **jigsaw.** Putting
the jigsaw box to one side, she
left the stew to boil.

An hour later the family sat down for a meal of jigsaw stew.

Jack couldn't face another spoonful of funny food. 'I don't feel well,' he said. 'I think the **wardrobe** we had for breakfast didn't agree with me.'

'That's ok,' said Mrs
MacAnoolie. 'You can eat your
stew later.'

They began their meal as Jack
left the table.

Molly was the first to finish. She had just licked her bowl clean when her stomach **growled**.

'Oooh! I think that jigsaw may have been off,' she said.

'Hmm,' said her mother. 'Jack, have a look at the jigsaw box. See if it has a sell-by date.'

Jack looked at the front of the box.
There was no date so he looked at the
back.

On the back he saw something
that puzzled him.

'What's **"Jigsalgia"**...?' he
asked.

Chapter 2

Jigsalgia attacks!

Mr MacAnoolie turned the pages of *The Family Health Encyclopaedia.*

'Here it is,' he said, 'JIGSALGIA: Rare illness. In which patient turns into a jigsaw and **falls apart**!'

Jack tried hard not to smile as he looked at Molly. Then he noticed something odd. Molly had become very quiet and **flat**.

'Serves her right,' he giggled.

Mr MacAnoolie grabbed his daughter. 'Nothing a good **shaking** wouldn't cure,' he said.

It didn't help.

Suddenly, a jigsaw-like pattern spread across Molly. Then,

She collapsed into a heap of two hundred jigsaw bits.

Mrs MacAnoolie shrieked. But, tidy as ever, she reached for the broom.

She had only just swept Molly into a corner when her broom hit the floor with a **BANG!**

When Jack turned to look, all
he could see was a jigsaw heap
where his mother
used to be.

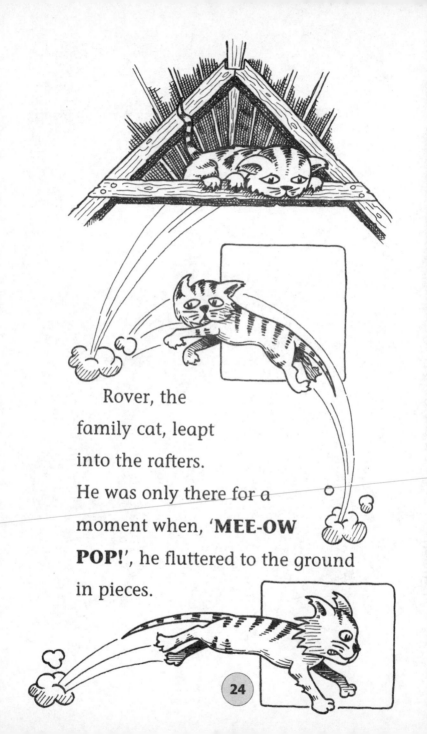

Rover, the
family cat, leapt
into the rafters.
He was only there for a
moment when, '**MEE-OW
POP!**', he fluttered to the ground
in pieces.

Jack's dad began to flatten. 'Get help!' he called to Jack. 'Get us to **Doctor Mulgrew**. He'll know what to do.'

Then **POP!** He was nothing more than bits of cardboard.

Jack was gripped with **panic**
and surrounded by **jigsaws**. He
knew he had to act fast.

After gathering all of the family into the jigsaw box, he opened the cottage door. The wind chilled him to the bone. He knew he might turn into an **ice-cube** out there. But if he wanted his family back in one piece, he would have to risk it.

Taking a deep breath, he
marched into the snow ...

Chapter 3

The Cardboard Snow Boat

Doctor Mulgrew lived four miles away. Jack had only travelled four feet when he realised he wasn't going to make it on foot.

He looked about desperately
for an idea. The icy wind chewed
on his nose. It pinched at his ears.
Finally it gave him the idea he
was looking for.

It was a simple matter of
taking off his **trousers** and
breaking a branch from a tree.

Using the trousers and branch, he made himself a very smart **sail** and waited for the wind to pick up. His knees were just beginning to chatter when …

A huge gust blew and Jack was on his way. He shot like a **cannonball** through the countryside – over hills, through forests and across frozen lakes.

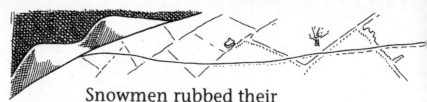

Snowmen rubbed their
piece-of-coal eyes when they saw Jack
coming. They jumped aside as he
rocketed past. Foxes panicked, gave
up looking for rabbits and leapt into
snowdrifts.

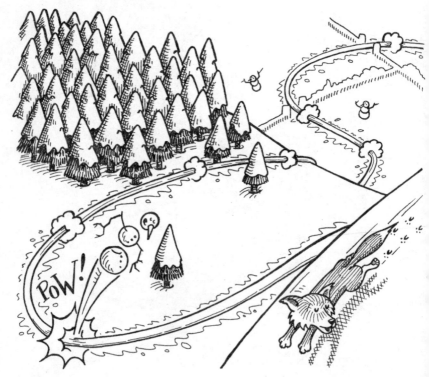

The wind blew on. The whole
countryside suddenly woke up to
the sight of Jack **thundering**
past.

Doctor Mulgrew's house came into sight.

'Almost there,' said Jack through gritted teeth.

The wind blew harder and he picked up speed. Jack's eyes watered. **Snow** flew in every direction. The house came closer.

Jack, the jigsaw box, the
branch and his trousers rattled
with blinding **speed** up to the
doctor's gate. It was only then he
realised ...

38

... the jigsaw box had no

brakes!

Doctor Mulgrew opened the door to see what the noise was.

He saw Jack without his trousers on. He saw Jack's trousers on the garden gate. He saw jigsaw pieces everywhere. He saw a soggy cardboard box.

Instantly he knew Jack needed **help**.

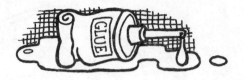

Chapter 4

The Mulgrew Mix-up

Doctor Mulgrew was clearly surprised.

'**Jigsalgia!**' he said. 'Quickly, we must pick up every single piece.'

'How did you know it was Jigsalgia?' asked Jack.

'I once cured a man who ate a whole jigsaw for a bet. Well, almost cured him – he had to go home **noseless.**'

Noseless?

'Yes, noseless,' continued Doctor Mulgrew. 'He arrived here by post. Somewhere on the way the jigsaw piece with his nose on it was lost. I put him back together, but without a nose. From then on he had to use a carrot instead. We cannot allow *anything* like that to happen this time.'

After carefully gathering all
the pieces, the pair went inside.

Jack was left in the waiting-room
while Doctor Mulgrew set to work.

Strange noises began to come
from behind the doctor's door. They
made Jack wonder exactly what was
going on.

After half an hour the doctor appeared.

'I have wonderful news,' he said. 'Your mother is **cured**!'

Jack looked towards the door …

'That's not my **mother**!!' he howled. 'Well, maybe bits of it are my mother. I can see some of my sister and father in there too.'

'Oh, you mean there is more than one person?' asked the doctor. 'That explains all the leftover pieces. Umm ... I think I shall have to start again.'

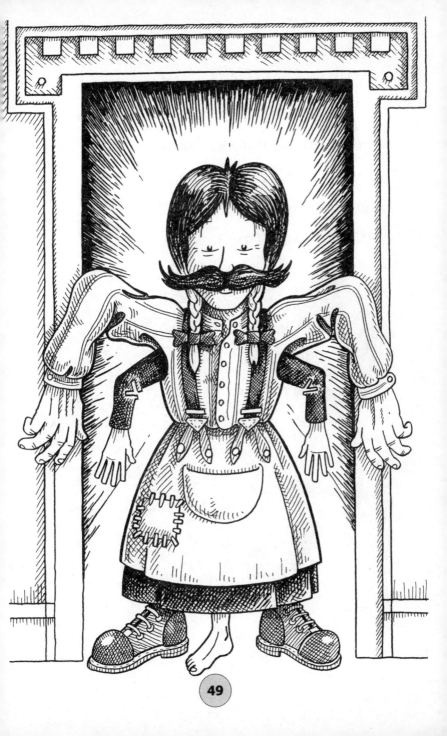

Doctor Mulgrew opened a jigsaw box and gave Jack's mother-mollyfather a few pieces. She swallowed them with a glass of water. Then **POP!** It was time to start again.

'All right, Jack,' said the
doctor. 'This time I need your
help. First we must assemble and
glue together each one of your
family.'

The pair set to work. Jack wondered if he could find the jigsaw piece which made Molly so **nasty** and leave it out. He was just about to start looking when Doctor Mulgrew interrupted. 'The cat's tail is **missing**!' he exclaimed.

They searched through the
gluey jigsaw pieces. They looked
on the floor. They emptied their
pockets. After an hour they gave
up.

'He will just have to do
without it,' declared Doctor
Mulgrew.

When all the family were assembled, Jack asked, 'What **next**?'

'Next,' said the doctor. 'We need this ...'

He was holding the most enormous **bicycle pump** Jack had ever seen in his life.

He put one end of the pump into Molly's ear and began pumping …

Chapter 5

Cured?

There were creaking noises. The doctor pumped harder. Molly began to **swell**. The doctor sweated. The pump hissed. The jigsaw pattern slowly began to disappear.

HiSSSSss

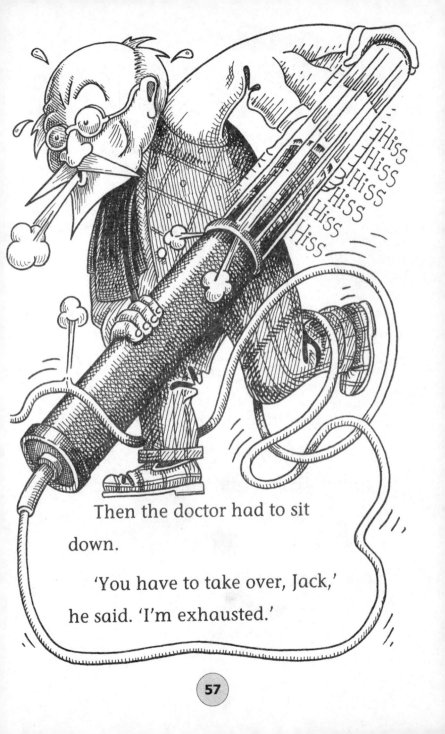

Then the doctor had to sit down.

'You have to take over, Jack,' he said. 'I'm exhausted.'

Jack pumped with all his heart. He noticed Molly's body was becoming round. He kept pumping. The last of the jigsaw pattern disappeared. Molly was starting to look like her old self again. With a huge effort, Jack gave one last pump.

Molly burped and her eyes
flickered to life.

'Jack, Jack, your teeth are
black!' she shouted.

'She's **cured**!' cried Jack.

Within twenty minutes, Mrs MacAnoolie was inflated back to normal. In another twenty, Mr MacAnoolie was too. And lastly, Rover sprang to life.

'I'm very proud of you son,' said Mr MacAnoolie.

'You're my hero,' said Mrs MacAnoolie.

'You're a big **cissy**!' said Molly.

Rover was too busy getting used to
life without a **tail** to thank Jack.
He examined himself in a mirror.
After that, he leapt about a bit to see
if he could still catch mice.

While he was doing this, Molly
took a good look at him. Roaring
with laughter, she said, 'A cat
without a tail ...'

'I can't think of anything more **daft**!'

The End